EMILY

DISASTER AT THE
BRIDGE

JULIE LAWSON

EMILY
DISASTER AT THE
BRIDGE
JULIE LAWSON

PENGUIN
CANADA

PENGUIN CANADA

Published by the Penguin Group

Penguin Books, a division of Pearson Canada, 10 Alcorn Avenue, Toronto, Ontario, Canada M4V 3B2

Penguin Books Ltd, 80 Strand, London WC2R 0RL, England

Penguin Putnam Inc., 375 Hudson Street, New York, New York 10014, U.S.A.

Penguin Books Australia Ltd, 250 Camberwell Road, Camberwell, Victoria 3124, Australia

Penguin Books India (P) Ltd, 11, Community Centre, Panchsheel Park, New Delhi – 110 017, India

Penguin Books (NZ) Ltd, cnr Rosedale and Airborne Roads, Albany, Auckland 1310, New Zealand

Penguin Books (South Africa) (Pty) Ltd, 24 Sturdee Avenue, Rosebank 2196, South Africa

Penguin Books Ltd, Registered Offices: 80 Strand, London WC2R 0RL, England

FIRST PUBLISHED 2002

1 3 5 7 9 10 8 6 4 2

COPYRIGHT © JULIE LAWSON, 2002
ILLUSTRATIONS © JANET WILSON, 2002
DESIGN: MATTHEWS COMMUNICATIONS DESIGN INC.
MAP & CHAPTER OPENER ILLUSTRATIONS © SHARON MATTHEWS

MANUFACTURED IN CANADA.

NATIONAL LIBRARY OF CANADA CATALOGUING IN PUBLICATION
Lawson, Julie, 1947-
Emily : disaster at the bridge / Julie Lawson.
(Our Canadian girl)
For ages 8-12.
ISBN 0-14-331206-5

1. Street railroads—British Columbia—Victoria—Accidents—Juvenile fiction.
I. Title. II. Title: Disaster at the bridge. III. Series.

PS8573.A933E453 2002   jC813'.54   C2002-901328-3
PZ7

Visit Penguin Canada's website at **www.penguin.ca**

For

Charlayne Thornton-Joe

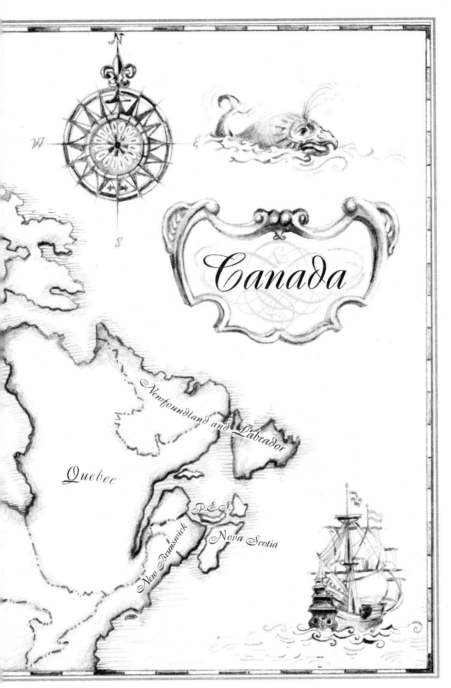

Canada

Newfoundland and Labrador

Quebec

P.E.I.

New Brunswick

Nova Scotia

 Marks the location of the story

INTRODUCTION

THE PLACE IS VICTORIA, BRITISH COLUMBIA, AND the time is late March, 1896. Emily's hometown was named for Queen Victoria, who has now been on the throne for nearly sixty years—as long as anyone can remember. Though Canada became a nation in 1867 and British Columbia has been a Canadian province since 1871, the ties to Britain are still strong.

The new craze in Victoria is bicycling, which has also introduced a bold new fashion—skirts that end a whole two inches above the ankle! Only the most daring cyclists are wearing them, provided that enough lead weights have been sewn into the hem to keep them from flying up in an unseemly manner.

We last saw Emily Murdoch in February, during the Chinese New Year celebrations. What an exciting time she had, collecting *lai see* envelopes filled with lucky money, visiting the shops in Chinatown, and attending the Chinese theatre with her family's cook, Hing. Like many of the Chinese people in Victoria, Hing has had to leave his family behind in China—including a daughter Emily's age—until he can save enough money to send for them. Emily decided to save some of her lucky money to buy a bicycle and to send some to Hing's daughter, Mei Yuk.

As the next chapter in Emily's story begins, she has much to look forward to—outings in the park with her best friend, Alice, the chance to compete on her school's running team, and the upcoming celebrations surrounding Queen Victoria's birthday on the 24th of May.

What does the spring of 1896 have in store? Turn the page and read on!

CHAPTER N° 1

"*Let's race to the top of the hill!*" *Emily* cried. She had been looking forward to this moment all afternoon, and not only for the joy of being outside with her friend, Alice. Earlier that day, the principal of her school had told her that she had a good chance of making the school's running team. The incentive made her run even faster.

It wasn't long before she'd outpaced Alice and reached the top of Beacon Hill. From there, it seemed as if she could see the whole world—sea, sky, mountains, rooftops, trees, and the hill stretching below like a lush green carpet sprinkled with blue camas lilies, buttercups, and purple shooting stars.

"You're too fast for me, Em," Alice gasped as she neared the top. "My heart's bursting!"

Emily extended a hand and pulled Alice the rest of the way. "You've made it! Now we can roll back down."

"I'll beat you this time," Alice said. "I'm much better at rolling."

They smoothed out their pinafores, lay on the grass and rolled down the hill, coming to rest in a patch of wildflowers. Laughing, they shook the leaves and blossoms from their hair and began to make spring garlands.

"George is moving away this week," Alice said. "His father bought a new house on the Gorge." Eleven-year-old George Walsh lived in Emily's neighbourhood, next door to Alice. He and his family had arrived not long ago from England, and Mr. Walsh worked with Emily's father at the bank.

Laughing, they shook the leaves and blossoms from their hair and began to make spring garlands.

"The Gorge?" Emily said wistfully. "They're so lucky. Some of the wealthiest people in Victoria live there. Father says the Gorge Waterway is the most beautiful part of the city."

"Do you know what else?" Alice continued. "I saw the people who bought the Walshes' house. They're moving in next Thursday, just in time for Easter."

"Do they have any boys?" Emily hoped another George wasn't moving next door to Alice. She did like George, and she would miss him, but his mischievous ideas had landed them both in trouble more than once.

"No, just one girl," Alice said. "I saw her yesterday. She's our age, very tall and pretty. And she was wearing fashionable clothes. I only saw her through my window so I didn't talk to her. But Tom was outside and he told me that when he said hello, she put her nose in the air and ignored him."

"She sounds like a snob," Emily said.

"Maybe, or she might be shy. Or maybe she

didn't like the look of my brother." Alice concentrated on weaving a few more camas lilies into her garland, then said, "Let's play the favourite game. And remember, you're not allowed to think. Just say the first thing that pops into your mind."

"I know the rules," said Emily. "You go first."

"Favourite place?"

"Beacon Hill. Favourite flower?"

"Easter lilies. Favourite food?"

"Hing's lemon tarts. Best friend?"

"You, of course!" Alice said. "Now, what do you want the most in the whole wide world? And don't say a bicycle."

"A bicycle bell."

"Be serious!" Alice laughed and threw a handful of shooting stars at her friend.

"Very well, then," Emily said. "What I want the most is for us to stay best friends forever."

"Me, too," said Alice. "Do you promise?"

"I promise," Emily replied.

They traded garlands to seal the bargain, then

linked arms and strolled through the park, stopping briefly to see the peacocks in their cages. After that, they parted company, Alice to go home, and Emily to meet her father at the James Bay Bridge.

There was a lot of traffic on the bridge—streetcars, horse-drawn hacks and carriages, people riding bicycles or walking. Emily scanned the crowd, hoping she hadn't missed her father by staying too long in the park. At last she spotted him and called out to get his attention.

He looked a little downcast, but his face brightened when he saw her. He smiled broadly, and Emily caught the familiar glint of his gold tooth. "You're early today."

"Good," she said, taking his hand. "I was afraid I might be late. See the flower necklace that Alice made?" She told him about rolling down the hill in the park and asked him about the Walsh family's move. "Would you like to live on the Gorge, Father?"

"Hmm? What's that about George?"

"Not George, Gorge!" She shook his arm impatiently.

"I'm sorry, dear. My mind's wandering."

Emily frowned. It wasn't like Father to be so absent-minded. "What's wrong? Did something happen at the bank?"

"Nothing for you to worry about." He plucked a stray buttercup from her hair. "Tell me about your day. You were saying something about the Gorge? How was school?"

She repeated what she'd already told him, then went on to say that school had been rather dull, except for the races.

"We're going to have running practice twice a week because there's going to be a sports day on the 24th of May, and all the schools in Victoria are taking part. Miss Cameron said that it will actually be on the 25th because the 24th is a

Sunday, but still, that's less than two months away. And Miss Cameron told me I had a good chance of running for South Park School because I won almost every race this morning."

"Well done!"

"George had a good chance too, but now he's going to be moving to another school. Miss Cameron said the races will be on the same day as the regatta, but in the morning, thank goodness! So we won't miss the regatta. And the day after that is the military tattoo. I can't wait until the 24th of May, can you?"

"No, that's one bright light to look forward to."

Only *one* bright light? Emily couldn't help but wonder what was troubling him. Ever since New Year's Day, when she'd heard her father talking to the other grown-ups about "tough times," his comment had gnawed at the back of her mind. What exactly did "tough times" mean? She'd recently overheard a neighbour telling her mother that he'd lost his job as a city worker because the city was hard pressed for money and could keep only a small staff. Then they'd started talking about "tough times" and "depression."

Whenever she asked her parents or their Chinese cook, Hing, about the situation, they told her not to worry. But she couldn't help it. It was one thing not being able to afford fancy new things, but what if "depression" meant something far worse?

She knew that something had happened to Father. All the way home he seemed preoccupied. His voice was quiet and his step wasn't as brisk as usual. And later, at supper, he scarcely said a word.

That night, when Mother came to tuck in the girls, Emily said bluntly, "What's the matter with Father?"

Her mother sighed. "He didn't get a promotion at the bank. He was expecting it, you see, and so he's very disappointed."

"Like when Emily didn't get a bicycle for her birthday?" asked four-year-old Amelia.

"Yes," Mother replied. "But pretty soon he'll feel better."

"Emily didn't."

"She did so!" eight-year-old Jane argued. "Didn't you, Em?"

Emily glanced up at the bicycle picture Jane had given her and nodded. She had felt better, eventually. But she still yearned for a bicycle. Just thinking about it made the knot of disappointment tighten up inside. If that was how Father was feeling, it was no wonder he was distracted. But at least he wasn't ill or dying or moving away. It wasn't the end of the world.

A few days later, Emily was curled up in the parlour, attempting to do some needlework, when Hing entered the room.

"Em-ry," he said, pronouncing her name as best he could.

Something in his tone told Emily she had better pay attention. She put down the needlework— the tiny stitches were giving her a headache anyway—and looked up. "What's wrong?"

"No!" Hing said. "Not *long*, not bad. *Good* news. Big change for me, you, family . . ."

He proceeded to explain.

Emily listened. Hing's news was hard to follow, and not only because of the confusing mix of l's for r's and r's for l's. Head tax, loans . . . restaurant, China . . . wife and sons and daughter . . . She couldn't take it all in, but one thing was clear. Hing was leaving.

"Why?" Her voice quavered. "I thought you liked it here. Oh, Hing, you *can't* go!"

"Today, last day of March," he said. "I give notice. Go two months, end of May. Em-ry . . . listen. Want own family here. And business. Friend go back to China, want to sell restaurant in Chinatown. I borrow money from Chinese merchant, buy restaurant. Pay head tax for wife and children. They come, work in restaurant. You come, eat in restaurant. Everybody happy."

"I'm not!" She burst into tears, flung the needlework onto the floor and ran outside, just as her father was coming up the path.

"Father, can't we persuade him to stay?" she cried.

"Don't I even get a hello?" he said. "Persuade who to stay?"

"Hing! He just told me he's leaving."

"Oh, dear. I'm sorry I didn't tell you, but with everything else . . . We'll miss him, of course, but it's a fine opportunity. Imagine, his own restaurant! Good for him."

"It's *not* good! What'll I do?" Hing was more than just a servant to Emily, he was a friend, a friend she'd known all her life. She couldn't imagine the house without him.

"Emily." Father took her hands and crouched down in front of her. "The world does not revolve around you or me or any of us, for that matter. If Hing has the chance to get ahead, I say good for him. And so must you."

That night, as Emily lay in bed, she thought about Hing and his family. Her mood brightened as she pictured their reunion. He hadn't seen them in ten years. And how happy he would be to meet his daughter, Mei Yuk, for the first time. Emily looked forward to meeting her too, especially since they were both born in the Year of the Dog. They were practically sisters! And maybe they could be good friends.

The next day, Emily hurried home from school to write Mei Yuk a letter. She gathered the necessary materials, dipped her brush in the thick, black ink, then bent over a sheet of paper, her face scrunched in concentration. Carefully, as Hing had taught her, she made the characters for "Mei" and "Yuk."

She had been practising calligraphy for weeks, other characters, too—like the ones for dragon and dog, mother and father. She didn't know enough for a whole letter, but at least she could begin with Mei Yuk's name.

Hing had told her that Mei Yuk meant

"Beautiful Jade." She wished her name meant something beautiful. Her mother had told her that Emily meant "industrious." Of all the dreary meanings for a name. Why couldn't it mean "swift" or "fast as lightning"?

Emily looked up as Hing entered the room and proudly showed him her calligraphy.

"Good!" He beamed. "Practice make perfect."

"I hope she writes back this time," Emily said. She had written to Mei Yuk during Chinese New Year and had enclosed a *lai see* envelope containing some lucky money, a New Year's gift. But she had never received a reply.

"Mail slow," Hing said. "Boat to Canton, China, take weeks. Then find village, take many days. Maybe letters pass in ocean. Em-ry go east, Mei Yuk go west!"

Emily smiled at the thought, then picked up a pencil and continued her letter.

Victoria, B.C.
Wednesday, April 1, 1896

Dear Mei Yuk (Beautiful Jade),

How are you? I hope you are fine.

In case you did not receive the letter I wrote in February, my name is Emily and your father is our cook. He told me that you are coming to live in Victoria. I hope you will go to South Park School and be in my class. I will help you learn English. Alice will help, too. She is my best friend.

Would you like to be called by your Chinese name or by your English name? Both names are very beautiful.

I hope someone in your village will read my letter to you.

I hope we will be friends.

Yours truly,
Emily Murdoch

CHAPTER №3

A frog, a log, and a dog . . . *Emily tightened* her grip on her pen and tried to concentrate on the day's lesson. But goodness, it was difficult. Especially on such a warm April day.

She leaned on her desk, chin in hand, and gazed out the window. She could hear the song of a red-winged blackbird and, every so often, the shrill cry of a peacock. As soon as school was out, she'd go to the park and feed the ducks. Maybe Alice would come . . . unless she was too busy with that *new* girl.

She groaned silently. The memory of her first meeting with Florence Featherby-Jones still rankled. It had taken place after church on Easter Sunday, when the whole neighbourhood had gathered in Beacon Hill Park for an Easter celebration.

The first event was an egg-rolling contest. Each child was given a coloured, hard-boiled egg and told to throw it down the hill. The one whose egg went the farthest got the prize.

Florence was put out because her egg didn't win. She was about to leave in a sulk when the Easter egg hunt was announced. There were eggs hidden everywhere—jelly eggs, cream eggs, hard-boiled eggs, and a few specially decorated chocolate eggs. Emily had just stumbled upon one of the chocolate eggs when Florence pushed her out of the way and grabbed it for herself.

And later, the way Florence had gone on about London, where she used to live, and the parties she'd attended at Buckingham Palace—only one, according to her mother—you'd have thought she was in line for the throne.

"Emily!"

Miss Lorimer's voice made her jump.

"Are you paying attention?"

"Yes, Miss."

"Well, then, sit *squarely* facing your desk. And mind how you're holding your pen. No wonder your writing is sloppy."

Florence snickered across the aisle.

"Hold your pen lightly," Miss Lorimer continued. "That's it, between the end of the thumb and the first two fingers."

Emily rolled her eyes but did as she was told. She hated her pen. It was long and straight and jumped out of her hand if she didn't keep a firm grip. And the metal nib made a sound more grating than the scrape of chalk on the blackboard.

A frog, a log, and a dog . . .

Six lines in her copybook. Six frogs, six logs, six dogs . . . What was the frog doing on the log? Who owned the dog? Was the log on the beach? Or near a bog? In the fog? She stifled a giggle.

She had almost finished when Florence leaned across the aisle and knocked over her inkwell.

"Oh, no!" Emily cried. She leapt up and grabbed her copybook, then opened the lid of her desk. A stream of ink was flowing through the crack, over her papers, pencils, copybooks, everything.

"I'm sorry," Florence said. She took a cloth from her desk and began to wipe up. "It was an accident. I only wanted to borrow your extra nib."

When the worst of the mess was cleaned up, Emily thanked Florence for helping, but she wondered if it really had been an accident. Florence hadn't been pleased when her mother had made her give Emily the chocolate Easter egg. Four days had gone by, but perhaps she was still holding a grudge.

As it turned out, Alice couldn't feed the ducks after school because she'd promised to go to Florence's house. Emily was invited to join them, but it wasn't long before she was wishing she'd gone to the park by herself.

"You know, Emily," Florence said as they were walking along, "your face is very red. It looks as though you wash it with strawberry juice. Don't you want your skin to be white? I do. That's why I'm a vegetarian. I eat no meat whatsoever."

Emily and Alice raised their eyebrows. "What do you eat?" Emily asked. "Don't you get hungry?"

"No," Florence replied. "For breakfast I eat oatmeal and oranges. For dinner I might have fruit and nuts, or cauliflower croquettes and stewed vegetables. And I drink fruit tea, preferably quince."

Alice pulled a face. "It sounds dreadful."

"My mother considers that caring for one's health and complexion is a duty," said Florence. Her tone clearly implied that *some* girls' mothers were failing in their duty. "You can improve your appearance, Emily. You too, Alice."

"There's nothing wrong with Alice's appearance," Emily said loyally.

"Or Emily's," said Alice.

"There's always room for improvement," Florence said. "But you have to abstain from bread and butter and sweets."

"I'd never give up sweets," said Emily. "And what about you and the Easter eggs? You weren't abstaining then."

"That was Easter," Florence said, as if that explained everything.

"What should we drink?" Alice wondered. "Besides quince tea."

"A glass of clear water every day before breakfast. Or lemonade."

"It's not too late, is it?" said Alice. "If we want to be as pretty as you?"

"Alice!" Emily's mouth dropped. Surely her friend wasn't serious.

"It's never too late." Florence smiled. "You know, when I was in London . . ."

By the time they'd reached Florence's house,

Emily had had enough. She made her excuses and hurried home, then looked in the mirror to see if Florence was right. Of course, her face turned red when she ran, or when she was embarrassed, but not all the time. As for strawberry juice? The nerve! She wished she could have told Florence how to improve her big teeth and gummy smile. Or how to get rid of her silly dimples.

She had to admit that the new girl was clever, though. She got perfect scores in spelling and almost perfect scores in arithmetic. Her penmanship was praised to the skies. And when the teacher asked a question, Florence always knew the answer.

Emily knew the answers, too—most of them, anyway—but the teacher always seemed to call on Florence.

"She thinks she knows everything," Emily complained to Alice one day. It was a Saturday, and they were sitting on top of Beacon Hill making daisy chains. "She's such a snob. She looks down on us, you know. I heard her say she was glad *she* wasn't born in the colonies. Doesn't she know Canada isn't a colony any more? And she says we don't speak proper English."

Alice gave a loud sigh. "Oh, Em! Don't let it bother you. I like Florence. She's a bit spoiled—"

"More than a bit!"

"But she tells funny stories and makes me laugh."

"They're not true."

"I know, but what difference does it make?" She placed her daisy chain on Emily's head. "This is your crown. Because you're still the best runner."

"Do you really think so?"

"Of course! Now let's play. Favourite subject?"

"Calisthenics. Favourite colour?"

"Blue. Favourite boy?"

"George."

"George?" Alice shrieked.

Emily clapped a hand to her mouth. "No! I

didn't mean George, I meant Father! What was I thinking?"

"Favourite candy?"

"Jawbreakers. Best friend?"

"Quince tea!" Alice hooted with laughter.

"What?"

"I'm joking, silly. You're my best friend."

Emily smiled, but for the first time ever, she felt a twinge of doubt.

CHAPTER Nº 4

"*Warm-ups first!*" *Miss Cameron said to* the assembled group. "Ten minutes jogging around the field."

Florence raised her hand. "Excuse me, Miss Cameron. I don't see the need for warm-ups. We never did them in London."

"But you're not in London now," Miss Cameron said, "and we don't want you to run the risk of pulling a muscle. Follow Emily's example. She knows the value of a good warm-up."

Emily set off at a light jog, pleased that Miss

Cameron, the principal, had singled her out.

There were twenty girls and boys in all. Today's session was to determine which pupils would make the final cut and compete in the 24th of May races, now four weeks away.

As they jogged around the field, Emily noticed Alice watching from the sidelines. "Good luck, Em!" she called out. "You too, Florence! I hope you both make the team!"

Emily weighed her chances. She was the youngest in the group, but one of the fastest sprinters. Florence was fast too, but why wouldn't she be? She was perfect at everything.

Before Florence arrived, there was no question of Emily not making the team. But now, if Miss Cameron had to choose between them . . .

Stop it! she scolded herself. *There's nothing you can do but try your best.*

It wasn't as though she hadn't been practising. Hing never had to beat the dinner gong at noon, because she was making it home in less than three minutes. Mother said she was so fast on her feet that she'd never need a bicycle.

She hadn't missed a single after-school practice and, in their daily calisthenics class, she worked harder than anyone. She'd learned to run on the balls of her feet and to lift her knees high to get longer strides. She'd also learned that the faster she swung her arms, the faster her legs would move. Her legs were short—much shorter than Florence's—but they were strong. Most important, she'd learned to ignore the runners on either side, because any distraction—a glance or even a passing thought—could cost precious time.

At the sound of Miss Cameron's whistle, she jogged back to the starting line. Stretching was the next part of the warm-up and, for once, Florence didn't feel the need to tell everyone how it was done in London.

Then it was time for the races. First, the 220-yard dash. Emily started fast, eased up a little, then drove for the tape at the end and came in fourth.

Florence was first. "You should have started your final burst a bit sooner," she told Emily.

"That's what I did."

There were a few races for the boys, and then for the older pupils. Finally it was time for Emily's favourite—the 100-yard dash.

"On your marks . . . Get set . . . GO!"

Emily's start was explosive. She flew down the track, knees high, arms pumping at her sides, her concentration focused on a point beyond the tape—and she made it first across the finish line.

Florence was a close second.

After everyone had caught their breath, Miss Cameron made her announcement. Emily waited anxiously as, one by one, the names were called out.

". . . Florence Featherby-Jones . . . and last but not least—usually first, come to think of it," Miss Cameron quipped, "Emily Murdoch."

"Hurray!" Alice ran over and gave each girl a hug, then invited them to her house to play hopscotch.

Emily said she couldn't because of her chores, but it was only an excuse. She hated playing games with Florence. If Florence won, she gloated, and if she lost, she sulked.

All the same, Emily felt left out as she watched the two girls link arms and walk off together. It made her realize that staying friends with Alice would mean making friends with Florence. She vowed to try.

Emily was doing her best to get along with Florence and felt that she was succeeding quite admirably—until the day Florence came to school with a bicycle.

Emily had never seen such a beautiful bicycle. It was a Raleigh, shipped all the way from England, with silvery spokes and chain, a red enamel finish, and a black leather saddle. It even had a brass kerosene lamp and a double-stroke bell with a pure, clear sound.

"You may think the colour is red," Florence told

her admiring classmates, "but it's not. It's vermilion."

"Vermilion," Emily murmured. Everything about the bicycle was perfect, even the name of the colour.

At lunchtime, Florence made a surprising offer. "Would anyone like to ride it?"

"Me! I would!" Everyone was shouting at once. "Please, Florence! Pick me!"

"Pick Emily!" said Alice. "She's longing for a bicycle. And she knows how to ride one."

Emily blushed. Where had Alice got that idea? She'd never actually ridden a bicycle. But it couldn't be that difficult, could it?

"Come on, then." Florence held the bicycle steady as Emily climbed on. "I'll push until we're out of the schoolyard."

Emily smiled. It felt wonderful.

Once they were on the street, Florence said, "Don't look down or you might lose your balance."

"She knows that," said Alice.

"The seat's a bit high," Emily said. "I can hardly reach the pedals."

Florence didn't seem to hear. She gave her a shove and stepped back.

"Wait!" Emily cried. "Don't let go, I'm not—"

"Keep pedalling!"

Emily tried. Before she knew it, the bicycle had hit a slope and was rapidly gaining speed.

"Brakes! Put on the brakes!"

Brakes? Where were the brakes? Emily had no idea how to stop a bicycle.

Everyone was running and yelling.

"Backwards! Pedal backwards!"

"Look out!"

"You're going to crash!"

In desperation, Emily pushed the top pedal backwards. The bicycle slammed to a stop. Over she went, in a flurry of skirts and spinning wheels, and landed in the bushes beside the road.

Tears stung her eyes. Her hands were grazed, she'd bitten her lip, and her bones ached from head to toe.

Florence was furious. "You crashed my bicycle! Don't you know they're coaster brakes? You're not meant to *jam* them!"

"Are you all right, Em?" Alice knelt down and offered Emily her handkerchief.

"I should never have let you ride it," Florence continued. "You said you knew how!"

Emily didn't bother to correct her. She just wiped her eyes with Alice's handkerchief and limped away with as much dignity as she could manage.

Back at the school, she went into the water closet, cleaned herself up, and cried.

"Emily?" It was Alice at the door. "Miss Cameron's about to ring the bell. You'd better hurry."

"Go away."

"Florence said she was sorry."

"I don't believe you. She hates me and I hate her. She's nothing but a—a *depression*." It wasn't the right word, but it summed up her feelings, as well

Before she knew it, the bicycle had hit a slope and was rapidly gaining speed.

as all the things that had been going wrong.

On the way to her classroom, Emily was stopped by Miss Cameron, who took one look at her scrapes and promptly led her to the medicine chest. "Can't have you injured for the 24th, can we?" she said. "There! A little witch hazel will do the trick." She dabbed the soothing lotion on Emily's hands and lip and asked what had happened.

"I was trying to ride Florence's bicycle," Emily said.

"Good for you! The only way to learn is by doing."

"But I didn't learn. I fell off."

"Never mind. Some people learn right away and others take longer. A few more lessons and you'll be on your way. And I promise you, once you learn how, you'll never forget. Now . . . feeling better?"

Emily nodded. Not that she'd ever have another lesson. Or a bicycle.

By the time she returned to her classroom, everyone was working on the spelling lesson. Last week, the lesson had been "What a Boy or Girl Should Be." This week, it was the opposite. Emily took out her copybook. With a shaky hand, still smarting from her fall, she wrote the heading and copied the words from the blackboard.

What a Boy or Girl Should *Not* Be:

bad

mean

proud

lazy

sulky

saucy

stingy

The list went on: selfish, fretful, profane, vicious, heedless, impolite, deceitful, dishonest, cowardly, quarrelsome.

As far as Emily was concerned, every word described Florence.

CHAPTER N° 5

Emily had seldom known an afternoon to pass so slowly. She tried to concentrate on her lessons, but all she could think about was the special tea she was having with Alice. They'd arranged it days ago, as soon as Emily had heard that her Friday practice was cancelled. It would be like old times, just the two of them, and this time, she would not mention Florence.

Finally the afternoon came to an end. Emily was gathering up her things, eagerly planning what they might do after tea, when she saw Alice and Florence leaving the cloakroom, arm in arm.

"Alice, wait!" she called. "Aren't you coming home with me? It's our tea, remember?"

Alice's face dropped. "Oh, no! I'm sorry, Em. I completely forgot. And yesterday I promised Florence . . ." She looked from one to the other, clearly embarrassed. "We were going to play her new board game, but now she's going to teach me to ride her bicycle." She whispered something in Florence's ear and Florence, after glancing at Emily, nodded grudgingly.

"You can come too," said Alice.

"No, I can't. I have to be home for tea."

"Well, then, come after tea. That's all right, isn't it, Florence?"

Mean, sulky Florence said nothing.

When Emily got home she found the tea laid out in the parlour, with settings for two and a plate of Hing's special lemon tarts. She took one look and burst into tears.

"Emily!" Her mother and sisters rushed into the room, followed by an anxious Hing. "What's wrong?" Mother said. "Where's Alice?"

"She went off with Florence!" Emily sobbed. "And now I don't have any friends."

"You have us," Jane said. "We'll stay for tea."

Emily managed a smile. Before long, another two places were laid.

"You can invite Alice another time," Mother said. "I'm sure she didn't forget on purpose."

"You stop worry," Hing said. "Think of race. Only two week away. I make special dish—rice for energy, and chicken—make you run fast, stay strong."

Emily sniffed. "Will it make Alice and Florence like me?"

"Ha!" Hing snorted. "They don't like you, they big loser. You winner. You born Year of Dog, remember? Like . . ." He thought for a moment. "Greyhound! Very fast."

Amelia giggled. "Emily's a greyhound!"

"Florence is a big bad wolfhound," said Jane.

"What am I?" Amelia wanted to know.

"You Pekingese!" Hing said, and everyone laughed.

After tea, Emily set off for the bridge as usual to wait for her father. On the way, she met Alice.

"I was coming to your house," Alice said. "Can I walk with you?"

"Where's your new friend?" Emily said bitterly.

"You could have come with us."

"No, I couldn't. Hing had everything ready for tea, and Florence didn't want me. And what would I have done? Stood around and watched while you rode her bicycle? I bet she didn't make *you* fall."

"No," Alice admitted. "Anyway, we spent most

of the time playing games. You should have come over after tea. She wants to be friends, you know."

"No, she doesn't. She doesn't even like me—and I know why. It's because I don't fawn all over her the way you do."

Alice stopped in her tracks. "I don't *fawn*."

"Yes, you do." Emily wished she could take back the words but it was too late. Before she could stop herself, she blundered on. " 'Oh, Florence,' " she mimicked, " 'you have such *pretty* hair. Your clothes are so *stylish*. You're so *clever*. You're such a good runner . . .' "

"I never said that."

"It's pathetic."

"Well, I like her, Emily. So there! And if you don't want to play with us, you can play by yourself." With that, she stormed away.

Emily watched her go, sick at heart. Alice had come to make amends and instead of being happy and grateful, she'd behaved in a rude, spiteful, despicable way. She was everything a friend should *not* be.

On Friday evening, after a whole week of being ignored by Alice, Emily sat down with paper and pencil and wrote Hing's daughter a letter. At least she had Mei Yuk for a friend.

Friday, May 15, 1896

Dear Mei Yuk,

I am sorry for not writing your name in calligraphy, but I am too upset to concentrate. Last week I had a fight with my best friend, Alice. I said mean things because I am jealous. Florence is pretty and clever and stylish. She is also a very fast runner, and she has a bicycle, and now she has Alice for her friend.

I promise that from now on I will try to be what a friend should be: kind, brave, noble, polite, honest, thoughtful, and loving. I will also be understanding, if you want to play with someone else sometimes.

Yours truly,

Emily Murdoch

Emily was reading over the words when it dawned on her—the letter should really go to Alice! Poor Mei Yuk would be so confused by such an outpouring of feelings that she might never want to hear from Emily again, let alone meet her. She erased Mei Yuk's name and wrote "Alice." Then, before she could change her mind, she put the letter in an envelope and ran outside to drop it in the letter box.

CHAPTER N° 6

"Why so quiet, Em? Oh, I know!" Jane grinned. "You're excited about seeing George!"

Emily rolled her eyes and refused to rise to Jane's bait. She had been gazing out the streetcar window, thinking about her letter to Alice. It would have been collected that morning and taken to the post office. There was no delivery tomorrow, being Sunday, but Alice might have the letter as early as Monday.

Her thoughts now turned to George. His parents had invited the Murdochs to their new

house on the Gorge for a pre-holiday picnic
and, although Emily was looking forward to the
picnic, she had mixed feelings about George. It
was almost two months since she'd last seen
him, and she couldn't help but wonder how he
might behave. Endless bragging, no doubt. And
teasing whenever he got the chance. Maybe
he'd dare her to do something reckless—like
jump into the freezing waters of the Gorge, or
spy on the neighbours. She began to brace
herself for what might be a long and unpleasant
afternoon.

She needn't have worried. George appeared
pleased to see her and her family and led them all
out to the garden for a picnic feast. Cold roast
beef, veal-and-ham pies, sliced tomatoes, bread-
and-butter sandwiches, stuffed eggs, pickles and
olives, cake and lemonade!

While they were eating, Emily gave George
the news about his former school and classmates,
and told him that she'd made the running team.

George grinned. "Then you'll be competing

against me in the 100-yard dash," he said. "Think you've got a chance?"

"I've beaten you before," Emily said. "Remember all those times at Beacon Hill? And that was running uphill!"

"Who else is on the team?"

"Florence, the girl who moved into your old house. She's really fast and she hates to lose." She was about to say more when George leapt up and shouted, "Roger!"

Emily turned and saw an older version of George walking towards them, dressed in a Royal Navy uniform.

"This is my brother, Roger," George said proudly. "He's taking part in the regatta on Monday and in the pageant on Tuesday, in the sham battle." He introduced everyone and, after a short time, the two wandered off together.

"What's a 'jam battle'?" Amelia asked.

"It's *sham*," said Emily. "It's pretend."

"But what does it mean?"

Emily swallowed her last bit of cake, then

jumped up and began to march. "I remember from last year, so I'll show you. You too, Jane. Come on, we'll play pageant. Hup, two, three, four! Order Arms! Shoulder Arms! Here come the Bluejackets!"

"What's Bluejackets?" asked Amelia.

"The Royal Navy, like Roger. Hup, two, three, four. Now, here come the Marines. And here's the Fifth Regiment. Hup, two, three—eyes front, Amelia. Jane, stop laughing. *Jane!*"

"I can't help it! Look at George!"

Emily turned and caught George imitating her behind her back. She blushed and was about to run off when Roger said, "Don't pay any attention to George, Emily. You make a fine officer."

His words made her blush even harder.

Amelia tugged on his sleeve. "Why don't you play too?"

"Amelia!" Emily glared at her sister. "He's a grown-up."

"We'll all play," Roger said. "Even George. He's never seen Victoria's famous pageant, and I've been rehearsing all week. File in, George."

After a few more rounds of marching, Jane asked Roger to tell them about the pageant.

"It's very thrilling," he explained. "First, there's a march past the Admiral with salutes and cannon fire. Then there are physical drills with sword-bayonets. Then the 5th Regiment mounts and dismounts the nine-pounders—those are the big guns—and after all that, there's the sham battle."

"And it's just pretend," said Amelia.

"Oh, yes. No one gets hurt. The Bluejackets try to reach the fort while the artillery tries to keep them away. Attack and defend, like in a real battle."

"But it's only pretend."

"Amelia!" Jane and Emily groaned.

Roger patted Amelia's head. "You are a worry-wart, aren't you?"

"No, Emily's the worrywart. That's what Father says."

"Worrywart!" George teased.

"I am not!" Emily protested, even though she knew it was true.

"It's all good fun," Roger went on, "but you have to keep well off the parade ground for your own safety. And so you won't interfere with the battle."

"And it's just pretend," said Amelia.

"Amelia!"

"Safe as houses!" Roger laughed. "Nevertheless, I expect to hear all of you cheering loudly for the Bluejackets on Tuesday. Can we count on you?"

Emily and Jane nodded vigorously, and Amelia piped up, "Can we practise now? Hurrah for the Bluejackets!"

"Hurrah for the Bluejackets," they all shouted, and they played pageant until it was time to go home.

CHAPTER  7

The rain was falling in sheets and the wind was blowing a gale. All day long Emily worried about the weather. Only two days until Sunday, the 24th of May, and three days until the start of the holiday. What if the weather didn't change? What if the school sports were cancelled? Or the regatta?

By the time she got home she was tired of worrying, and pushed the "what ifs" out of her mind. It could rain all it liked, at least until Monday. Now she had something else to think about.

She dipped her brush in the ink and wrote Mei Yuk's name. The calligraphy made her smile. Alice had received her letter on Tuesday afternoon and had come right over to Emily's house. After giving Emily a hug and saying she was sorry too, she'd asked, "What's calligraphy? It's the only part of your letter I didn't understand." Emily had promised to teach Alice what little calligraphy she knew.

Victoria, B.C.
Friday, May 22, 1896

Dear Mei Yuk,

How are you? I am feeling much better than I did a few days ago. I had a terrible fight with my best friend, Alice, but we both apologized and made up. I told her about the letters I'm writing to you, and she says she hopes that we can all be friends.

In three days I will be running in some races. Hing made me a special soup. He said it was made with chicken feet, because chickens run fast, but I think he was joking (about the feet). He is a very good cook and his new restaurant is going to be very nice. He said I could help him think of a name, but it has to be a lucky name. I think he is lucky already because soon he will see his whole family.

After the races there is a regatta with lots of boats. We are going in a boat parade at night and Hing gave me a Chinese lantern especially for the occasion.

Please write back to me.

Yours truly,
Emily Murdoch

She sighed, saddened by the thought of Hing. He was leaving at the end of May, only one week away. It would be different at home without him, and she was glad she had the holiday to take her mind off his leaving. He'd told her that he was glad too, because he would miss her very much.

Earlier that week, her family had gone to Chinatown to see his restaurant. It was in a brick building near Fan Tan Alley, very small, but nicely decorated with lanterns and pictures of dragons.

Remembering this, she suddenly had an idea. She reached for a new sheet of paper and eagerly began to apply the brush strokes.

By Sunday night, the worst of the rain was over. Emily lay in bed, too excited to sleep, and said a few extra prayers for a fine, sunny day on Monday. She also said a prayer of thanks that she and Alice were friends once more.

"Em?" Jane whispered. "Are you awake?"

"Yes," Emily whispered back.

"I hope you win tomorrow. I hope you win every single race."

CHAPTER N°. 8

The moment had arrived. Emily stood at the starting line, her heart pounding. She'd won the 220-yard dash, beating Florence by a nose. Now it was time for the final event and the greatest challenge—the 100-yard dash.

The stands were packed. In spite of the cool, cloudy weather, people from all over Victoria had turned out to watch the public school sports at Beacon Hill. Emily's whole family was there, even Hing. How proud they would be if she could take home the blue ribbon for this race!

"On your marks!" the starter boomed.

Emily squatted down and positioned her hands behind the line. She gazed at the track in front of her, took a few deep breaths and tried to relax.

"Get set!"

She gathered herself for the start. Crouched and ready, she waited for the gun.

BANG!

She shoved off hard and thrust forward, aiming herself straight down the track with a smooth and rhythmic stride. Then, without thinking, she glanced over her shoulder.

Florence was gaining on her.

Come on, Em! She pushed herself harder, pumped her arms, and drove her legs to maintain her speed. Almost there—

Suddenly, she stumbled. She fought to keep from falling, but before she knew it she was on the ground.

She caught her breath and struggled to her feet. Tears welled up, from hurt pride as much as from sore knees. She could see from the crowds milling about that the race was over, but she hadn't finished. After brushing away the tears, she ran her best across the finish line.

Friends and family gathered around to make sure she was all right.

"What happened?" Alice said. "You've never fallen before."

"I'm fine," Emily assured everyone. "I don't know what happened. One minute I was up and the next minute . . ." She smiled sadly. "Who won?"

"George came in second," Jane said, "and another boy from Victoria West came third. Florence came first."

"Where is Florence?" Emily looked around but Florence was nowhere to be seen.

"She won," George said, "but it wasn't an accident when you stumbled. I saw her push you with her elbow. She cheated!"

"No!" Alice said. "She wouldn't dare!"

"Well, she did. I told the teachers. They asked her and she denied it. But where is she now?

Probably gone off with a guilty conscience."

"I'll find out," Alice said.

Emily swallowed hard. Had she been pushed? The slightest nudge would have set her off balance. And Florence had been so close. What should she do? Confront Florence directly? Her reaction would surely reveal something.

Moments later, when she saw Florence leaving the field with her parents, she lost her nerve. All she could say was, "Congratulations."

Florence's face turned crimson. When she turned away without speaking, and with no sign of her usual haughtiness, Emily was convinced that George was right.

"You've done a fine job today," Father said as they were walking home. "And crossing that finish line, even though the race was over—what spunk!" He gave her a hug. "Don't be sad. There'll be plenty of other races."

"But Florence pushed me. It wasn't fair."

"It was mean," Jane said. "Something bad should happen to her."

Emily agreed.

"Now, girls," Mother said. "It may well have been an accident. I think we should set the matter aside and not let it spoil our day. What do you say, Emily?"

"I'll try," she said.

By noon, when the royal salute was fired to announce the beginning of the regatta, she had almost put it out of her mind.

"Everything that floats is here!" Emily exclaimed as she and her sisters ran down to the shore. Father and Mother followed with rugs, cushions, and picnic baskets, and George and his parents weren't far behind. Before long, two cloths were spread out on the lawn and everyone was tucking into their picnic.

The Murdochs had once again been invited to the Walshes' home, this time to watch the regatta.

Mr. Walsh had even offered his rowboat for their return trip.

All thoughts of the race were put aside as Emily munched on a cold chicken leg and viewed the scene. The two barges at the head of the course were already filling up with regatta officials, and overhead, stretching from shore to shore, a line of colourful pennants snapped in the breeze.

On neighbouring lawns and along the wooded banks of the Gorge, hundreds of people were laying out their picnic lunches. Small fires were being built to boil water for tea, and hammocks were strung between trees. Some youngsters were wading into the water for their first swim of the year, although it was bitingly cold. Emily had not ventured more than a toe.

Decked with flags and streamers, the boats sailed up the Gorge, from the Inner Harbour, under the Point Ellice Bridge, and on to the head of the course—punts, rowboats, dinghies, sailboats, dugout canoes, and yachts. Many people who didn't have their own boats were coming by barge, towed by a steam-powered launch.

Even before the races started there was entertainment on the waterway. Lightweight sculls crashed into heavier boats, paddlers got drenched by the wash of the barges, and some rowboats were so overloaded they looked as if they might sink.

By the time Emily was finishing her strawberries and cream, the cutters and galleys of the Royal Navy were heading up to the starting point. Emily recognized Roger among the crew and called out a hearty greeting.

Just then, the sound of a bugle announced the first event—the single-paddle canoe race. The contestants lined up at the starting point, the cannon roared, and off they went, paddling feverishly to Point Ellice Bridge and back.

One race after another—sculls, cutters, canoes, four oars, ten oars, twelve oars—Emily could scarcely keep track.

She cheered the loudest for the Royal Navy. They had the heaviest boats and the longest course, two and a half miles, all the way from the starter's barge and around Deadman's Island.

Next to the Royal Navy contests, her favourite events were the Indian races. The Indians paddled forty-foot war canoes, with thirteen paddlers going like fury and the canoes so close together there was hardly any clear water between them. The Indian women, in their turn, paddled as furiously as the men.

The regatta was so thrilling, Emily had all but forgotten the incident with Florence—until Jane brought it up. They were watching a canoe race when one of the paddlers broke a blade and the others, instead of dashing on, stopped to throw him a spare. When they started a second time, another contestant fell into the water. The man who'd broken his paddle jumped in and helped him get back into the canoe.

"That's what Florence should have done when you fell," Jane said. "She should have stopped and helped you up, like a good sport. That's what you would have done if she'd fallen, isn't it, Em?"

Emily hesitated. She wanted to think that she would have been a good sport and done the right thing. But with Florence . . .

Fortunately, the start of the greasy-pole contest kept her from pursuing the matter. To many, it was the highlight of the afternoon. Eight sailors had lined up for the chance to win the prize—a few silver dollars and a little black pig hanging in a bag at the end of a long, slippery pole that stretched out over the water. As one sailor after another received a dunking, Emily's hopes soared for the pig.

Then the last sailor went out on the pole. Step by step, tottering here, lunging there, but still keeping his balance, he reached the end. To the cheers of the crowd, he removed the bag from the pole and belly-flopped into the water, his squealing prize in hand.

Daylight faded quickly after the final event, but the best part was yet to come—the illuminated boat parade.

The steam launch was ready and waiting. On its return to the Inner Harbour, it was towing not only the barge of holiday-makers but also all the boats taking part in the parade. One by one, the boaters arranged their crafts behind the barge.

At the sound of a gunshot, hundreds of paper lanterns hanging from the barge were lit. Lamps and torches glowed from every boat. Father lit Emily's Chinese lantern and gave it to her to hold.

Slowly and silently the procession moved over the water. Lanterns shone on both sides of the Gorge, from bridges, porches, and verandahs. A huge bonfire burned on Deadman's Island. The water gleamed with reflected light.

"It's like magic," Emily whispered. She looked up in awe as they approached the Point Ellice Bridge, where hundreds of people stood with blazing torches. As the floating pageant drifted beneath the bridge, the crowd began to sing "God Save the Queen."

Emily sang with all her heart. "Send Her victorious, happy and glorious . . ."

She hugged the glorious feeling all the way home.

CHAPTER N⁰ 9

"Is the whole world taking the streetcar?"
Emily frowned, worried that there might not be
enough room for everyone. The streets were
packed with people, all heading towards the main
streetcar station to get on a car for Esquimalt. No
one wanted to miss the military tattoo.

"Don't fret," Father said. "Every car available
has been pressed into service. There'll be plenty
of room."

Emily wasn't convinced. When they finally
reached the station she saw that two cars were

already filling up with passengers. "Are you sure there's space for all of us?"

"It might be a squeeze," Father admitted. "Stay close and we'll see."

He was about to usher the family onto Car 6 when the conductor said, "I'm afraid there's only room for four, sir. If you all want to stay together, you'll have to take Car 16. It's bigger, but you'd still better hurry."

Just then, Emily caught sight of Alice and her brother, Tom, waiting in line for the larger car. Alice saw her too.

"Emily, come with us!" she called.

"Can I, Father?" Emily asked. "Please?"

Father thought for a moment. "Very well," he said. "Hing can go with you. Here's the fare. We'll wait for you on the other side."

"Thank you!" Emily kissed him and her mother, said goodbye to her sisters, and ran off with Hing to join Alice.

Car 16 was every bit as crowded as Car 6. Once on board, the girls scrambled to the front while Tom climbed onto the roof. Hing decided to stay outside on the streetcar's rear platform.

More and more people clambered on board. Soon the platform was so packed that Emily lost sight of Hing. She was looking back, straining to find him, when she spotted Florence pushing her way through the crowd.

Emily's happy mood vanished. She whirled around and slouched down in her seat, praying that Florence would stay at the back of the car and not see them. Wasn't it enough that Florence had ruined her race? Did she have to ruin this part of the holiday too?

"Alice!" Florence's voice rose above the clamour and caught Alice's attention. Before Emily could stop her, Alice was waving and shouting, "Florence! Come up here!"

"There's no room," Emily muttered.

"There is if you move closer to the window," Alice said. "And it's important, because I talked to Florence yesterday about the race and she admitted the whole thing. She promised to tell you herself, and if she doesn't . . ."

Behind her, Emily could hear Florence saying, "Alice! I'm so glad—" Then her tone changed abruptly. "Oh . . . I didn't see Emily. I'm sorry. I'll go back and sit with my father."

"Stay here!" Alice pulled Florence onto the seat. "Remember what you promised. Go on, tell her! Or else I'll never speak to you again."

Florence leaned across Alice and, in a halting voice, said, "Emily . . . I'm sorry. About the race and . . . everything."

At that moment, the streetcar started up. The bell clanged and people's voices rose in anticipation.

Emily stared out the window and pretended she hadn't heard Florence. Soon they'd be in Esquimalt and she'd be with her family. Until then, she wanted to forget about the race and enjoy the streetcar ride with Alice. Maybe tomorrow she and Florence could make a fresh start at being friends.

As they were nearing the Point Ellice Bridge, the car slowed down to let Car 6 cross over first. It was stifling inside, with the afternoon sun beating through the windows and so many bodies pressed together. Emily asked the conductor to open her window, then leaned out as far as she could to breathe in the fresh air.

Up ahead, the bridge was busy with traffic. She counted three horse-drawn carriages and several people on foot. And there was George, coming up the street on his bicycle. "Alice, look!" she said. "George is going to bike across. He never told me he had a bicycle."

Alice leaned out beside her and the two waved excitedly. "Hello, George! We'll get there before you do!"

A man in the seat behind pulled out his pocket watch and grumbled, "It's ten minutes to two. Can't this car go any faster?"

"I can see Car 6," Emily said. "It's just reached the other side."

"About time," said the grumbler.

Slowly, Car 16 rolled onto the bridge. "We'll be lucky to get over with this load," the conductor remarked.

Emily took no notice of his words. What an adventure, taking the streetcar over the Gorge. And how brave of George to go on his bicycle. She was about to say as much to Alice when she heard a loud crack, like a gunshot. Her stomach lurched. Suddenly afraid, she reached for Alice's hand.

Then a second explosive crack split the air. Emily felt herself falling. The world turned into a terrifying confusion of arms and legs and bodies as the streetcar dropped through space and crashed into the water below.

Everything was dark.

Emily scarcely knew which way was up or down, but the car was underwater and water was pouring in and she knew she had to get out. Something was holding her—she wrenched herself free and, flailing her arms, discovered the open window above her head. She kicked her way out, then swam up through the water, desperate to reach the surface. Almost there—she had a sense of light—but then her head bumped against something and she was forced back down.

She tried again. The water was muddy, murky, filled with debris, but this time she reached the surface. With lungs bursting, she gasped for air and gulped it in. A fragment of the shattered car floated by. She lunged for it and held on. All around her, people were groaning and screaming, or floating silently, jammed between pieces of broken ironwork or timber.

A leg rose up beside her—a girl's leg, with a white stocking and a black button shoe. Struggling to keep a grip on the floating wreckage, Emily used her free hand to turn the girl upright, then gasped in horror. Florence! But was she dead or alive?

She couldn't look, she couldn't think. Frantically she pulled Florence onto the wreckage. She tried to hold on but no longer had the strength. All she could do was close her eyes and let go.

She tried to hold on but no longer had the strength. All she could do was close her eyes and let go.

CHAPTER N.º 10

Emily's thoughts drifted like ghosts, appeared and disappeared in a hazy world of water and light. She was lying in a boat, but who was rowing? Was it George? No . . . George was riding across the bridge. The bridge fell. George fell. Everyone fell.

She thought she could hear muffled cries and moans. She wanted to cry out—for her mother and father and sisters, for Hing, for Alice . . . She moved her lips and tasted salt. She tried to speak, but all she could manage was a moan.

Her teeth chattered. She couldn't stop shivering. She couldn't think why the sun felt so cold. Was she a ghost?

Water splashed beneath the oars. The rhythm lulled her into a drifting sleep.

The next thing she knew, Emily was lying on the ground, wrapped in a velvet curtain. People were moving about—hundreds, it seemed—and their voices were rising and falling around her.

"My daughters!" someone wailed. "Tell me, what's happened to my daughters?"

Someone else cried, "No, it can't be! My brother was right beside me!"

Then, "Alice! She can't be dead!"

Emily sat up abruptly. The blood rushed to her face and her pulse thudded in her ears. She remembered—the car, the bridge, the crash.

She remembered how she, Alice, and Florence had clasped each other, terrified, as the car went falling through space. Then it had tipped. Water had rushed in and she'd gone through the window, narrowly escaping the crush of people trying to get out the same way. She had left Alice behind. And Florence—but she'd seen her again. The button shoe, the wreckage . . .

She shuddered, stunned by what had happened. People were everywhere, lying or sitting on the ground, wandering about with dazed expressions, moving anxiously from person to person. She saw a row of bodies at the water's edge, young and old, men, women, and children. She turned away quickly, only to see the undertaker's wagon draw up at the gate.

A young woman came and knelt beside her. "What's your name, dear?"

Emily told her, then asked, "Who are you? Where am I?"

"I'm Miss Drake," the woman said kindly. "You're at Captain Grant's house and it's been turned into a hospital. They came that quick, the doctors. Other people, too, from all around, bringing clothes and blankets to help out. And when we ran out of blankets, Mrs. Grant took down her curtains, velvet and all." She wrapped the curtain more snugly around Emily and took her by the hand. "Come with me. We'll have a doctor look at you and find you some dry clothes."

"I want my mother." Emily started to cry. "Where's my mother?"

"Was she with you in the car?"

"No . . . only Alice and Florence. And Hing." Her body shook with tears.

"There, there." Miss Drake hugged her. "You've had a terrible shock, but now you're safe. You were lucky that boy came along when he did. I saw you slip under, but before I could reach you, he pulled you into his boat and brought you to shore."

As she was talking, Miss Drake was leading Emily towards the house. They'd almost reached the door when Emily looked over her shoulder and cried, "Hing!"

She ran across the lawn and into his outstretched arms. "You're alive?" she sobbed. "You're not a ghost?"

"No ghost," he said. "I fall, land in water. See? Clothes all wet! Hold on timber. Boat pick me up. Now you go in house. See doctor. Then we go home."

A short time later, Emily was in dry clothes and ready to leave. "I've got a bump on my head and some bruises," she told Hing. "The doctor said I was lucky."

"Very lucky," Hing said. "Many people not so lucky."

One of Captain Grant's neighbours offered them a ride home in his buggy. As they were driving by the approach to the collapsed bridge, they saw a huge gathering of people—some eager to be helpful, some frantic with anxiety, others in a state of shock. Emily and Hing scanned the crowd, hoping to catch a glimpse of her parents.

"Where are they?" Emily asked anxiously. "How will they know we're all right?"

"They'll have to cross back over on the railway bridge," their driver explained, "seeing as how they made it to the other side. I'll go back that way later and see if I can find them, let them know you're safe and sound."

As soon as they got home, Hing ordered Emily to drink some hot beef broth and promptly put her to bed.

"I'm not sleepy," she said. "I want to see Mother and Father."

"Sleep!" he said. "Family home soon. You wake up, you see."

"Hing . . . why did it happen?"

He didn't have an answer.

Emily tried to stay awake but couldn't. The last

thought she had before falling asleep was of the regatta, bright with colour and music and celebration. It already seemed like a lifetime ago.

It was noon the next day when Emily woke up. Jane and Amelia had clearly been watching and waiting, for the moment she opened her eyes they cried, "She's awake!" and hugged her.

Mother and Father rushed in and did the same.

At first, Emily was confused. "Am I late for school? What's—? Oh." She burst into tears. "Alice!" she cried. "I left Alice!"

"Alice is fine," Father said.

"She can't be! I heard someone say that she's dead!"

"No, dear. They must have meant another Alice. Your Alice is fine, except for a broken ankle. She got out the window after you but was hit by a piece of ironwork. A man picked her up and held her afloat until they were rescued. I saw her this morning. She's asking after you."

Emily sighed with relief. "And Florence?"

Her parents exchanged glances. "She's alive," Mother said. "And we've heard it's thanks to you. So Florence is fine . . . but her father was killed. Poor soul, he couldn't get out of the car."

CHAPTER N° 11

On the Friday following the disaster, George and his parents came to call. And Emily learned that it was George who had saved her.

"But how?" she wondered. "I saw you on your bicycle."

"I'd just got onto the bridge when I heard the first crack," he explained. "Then I pedalled like mad to get off. I biked straight over to Captain Grant's place—it's right there at the bridge—and went out in his rowboat. He was already rescuing people with the men from his sealing schooner, using his company's boats.

"You know, there was a horse and buggy in front of me on the bridge, and that horse must have sensed something. Because even before I heard the crack, it wheeled around and ran back to the city side. Got there safely, but the buggy just ahead of it went down with a whole family. And Tom! You know he was on the roof of the car? Well, he was thrown off and landed in a clear patch of water. No wreckage in the way, nothing. He just swam to shore."

"We're hearing of so many miracles," George's father said. "Two people sitting side by side on the car, one drowns, the other escapes with no injuries whatsoever. And those poor people sitting on the left-hand side of the car, like Mr. Featherby-Jones . . ." He shook his head sadly. "They had no chance at all once the car tipped over."

"And heroes!" said George's mother. "The number of people who rushed to help, like our George, and Justice Drake's daughters, fine ladies working side by side with rough men from the shipyard. And many people who were thought to have drowned were resuscitated in the nick of time. Three Chinamen were rescued too, like your Hing. But oh, mercy, the lives lost, old and young alike . . ."

Emily looked up and caught her father gazing at her, his eyes bright with tears. She couldn't imagine what might have happened if her whole family had taken Car 16. And to think that they had seen the car go down, knowing that she was on board . . .

Father held out his hand. "Let's go and feed the ducks," he said. "Jane and Amelia, you can come too."

Normally, the girls would have skipped or run to the park, chatting and laughing all the way. Today they walked in silence.

A gloom had settled over the city. There wasn't a single person who wasn't affected in some way, who didn't know someone who had lost a loved one. Many houses had a black wreath on the door, a sign that the family within was mourning a lost parent or child. Flags that had fluttered so gaily on the morning of the disaster now drooped at half-mast. Except for a funeral procession of hearses and carriages on their way to the cemetery, the streets were empty.

They found the park deserted, but it wasn't long before they were surrounded by ducks and swans, eager for a handout. A mother duck paddled towards them, followed by a string of eight ducklings, desperate to keep up. Emily was surprised to catch herself laughing. Father laughed too, and his gold tooth gleamed in the sun.

In the days following the tragedy, everyone had a story to tell about a narrow escape. No one could explain why some people had been saved while others had not. But there was a clear explanation for the cause of the disaster.

"The city and its cost-cutting measures!" Father said one evening. "The Depression is no excuse. One inspector, with one month's experience, and how does he examine the bridge? First he rows under and then—"

"Father, please stop," Emily said. "I don't want to hear about it."

His face softened. "Of course you don't. I'm sorry. I do have some happier news. Hing has agreed to stay on until the end of June. He wants to make sure you're really all right. Otherwise, he says, he'll be worrying about you and not paying attention to his restaurant."

Emily smiled. The end of June was a whole month away.

CHAPTER 12

Emily peeked through the kitchen doorway and watched Hing give the copper kettle one last shine. He had served his final meal at the Murdochs' home and done the washing up. Soon he would leave their house for the last time. But not before Emily gave him her surprise.

A few moments later, Father called Hing into the parlour. "We're sorry to see you go," he said. "But we wish you much prosperity, long life, and happiness." He handed Hing an envelope.

"And we have presents!" Amelia said excitedly.

With Jane's help, she unrolled it carefully, then held it up for Hing to see.

"Show him, Emily!"

Emily reached for the red scroll lying on the table. With Jane's help, she unrolled it carefully, then held it up for Hing to see.

"It's for your restaurant," she said. "I hope you like the name. I did the calligraphy and Jane drew the dragon and the clouds."

"I coloured his scales," said Amelia.

"Ah, Em-ry." Hing's voice was filled with emotion. "Jane, Amelia—thank you. Mei Yuk Lung! Beautiful Jade Dragon! Perfect name for restaurant. Very lucky. Hing lucky, too. You good girls. Very special."

Try as she might, Emily couldn't hold back the tears.

"Don't cry!" Hing said. "You come visit in restaurant. Use chopsticks. You fast runner, you come on time. Promise?"

Emily promised and said, "You'll never have to beat the gong for me again."

Something was different. Something about Father.

Emily thought about this as she weeded the vegetable garden. She had first sensed it the day after Hing left. What with his leaving and school ending, she hadn't pursued the matter, but all week long it had bothered her. It was something small, but somehow important.

She had more chores to do now that Hing was gone, especially since he was not being replaced. But after helping Mother with the cooking and baking and so forth, she still had time to enjoy her summer holidays. She and Florence had been keeping Alice company since school ended, playing games and having tea parties. Alice's ankle was mending nicely, and soon she would be able to join them on walks to the park and to the beach.

With everything that had happened, it was impossible for Emily to hold a grudge against Florence. Besides, Florence wasn't really so bad, once you got to know her.

Emily also had George's birthday party to look forward to. But how would she feel, going back to the Gorge?

George had told her that he sometimes saw lights flickering across the water at the scene of the tragedy. And on nights when the waterway was empty, he thought he could hear the splashing of oars and the plaintive cries of children.

Emily shivered. If things had been different, if she and Alice had sat on the left side of the car instead of the right, if Hing hadn't stayed outside on the platform . . .

Just then, she noticed Florence riding up to her house. She left the weeding and walked over to greet her.

"I can't stay," Florence said, "but I wanted to give you this. The seat's too high for you but you can lower it."

"What?" Emily stared at the bicycle. "You don't mean—"

"Yes, you can have it," Florence said. "We're moving back to England next week, Mother and I. The house has been sold." She handed the bicycle to Emily. "It won't take you long to learn how to ride it. Just make sure you have someone holding on for a while."

"I don't know how to thank you," Emily said.

"Me either," said Florence, smiling, and she held out her arms for a hug.

Later that afternoon, Emily wheeled the bicycle down to the James Bay Bridge and waited for her father. The moment she saw him, she waved and called out, "Look, Father! Florence gave me her bicycle!"

His reaction took her by surprise. Instead of saying, "How splendid," or "Lucky girl," he threw his head back and laughed.

In that instant, Emily knew what was different. "Your tooth! Where's your gold tooth?"

"Oh, Emily!" He ruffled her hair. "You'll see soon enough."

When they got home he leaned her bicycle against the side of the shed, opened the door, and went inside. A moment later he came out with a royal-blue Rambler. "This is for you."

"Father! I thought . . . You always said we couldn't afford it."

"Yes, but the disaster at the bridge got me thinking. I knew how much you wanted a bicycle. And you are that precious, I decided you must have one, tough times or not. So I pulled together almost enough money, then sold my gold tooth to make up the difference."

"But your smile looks different, and I loved your gold tooth. And two bicycles! What will I do with two?"

"Keep one, give one away. You decide."

It was an easy decision. She pointed to the vermilion Raleigh and said, "I'll give that one to Alice and I'll keep the Rambler. But only if you teach me how to ride it."

His smile warmed her heart, even without the gold. "Hop on," he said. "I'll hold it steady and make sure you never fall."

HISTORICAL NOTE

With fifty-five men, women, and children dead, and twenty-seven seriously injured, the streetcar disaster in Victoria on May 26, 1896, was an appalling tragedy. What made it even worse? It could have been prevented.

Car 16 was designed to carry sixty passengers, but on that day it carried over 140. The maximum weight that the bridge could bear was ten tons, but the estimated weight of the overloaded car was more than twice that amount.

Several survivors of the tragedy heard conductor Harry Talbot remark that they'd be lucky to get over the bridge with such a heavy load. He spoke from experience. Strangely enough, in 1893, he'd been the motorman in charge of Car 16 when, on the same holiday, the same bridge sagged four feet under the weight of the car.

After that near-disaster, boreholes were drilled to inspect the wooden beams. The holes were never filled. For three years, water collected inside and contributed to the rot that led to the ultimate collapse of the bridge.

The inspection that took place less than a month before the tragedy involved little more than a cursory look at the vibrations of passing traffic. Sadly, the inspector's five-year-old son was among the dead.

In the end, the City of Victoria and the streetcar company were found to be equally responsible. It was the worst streetcar accident ever to occur in North America.

Dear Reader,

Welcome back to the continuing adventures of Our Canadian Girl! It's been a very exciting year for us here at Penguin, publishing new stories of eight different girls, with more on the way! The best part of this past year, though, has been the wonderful letters we've received from readers like you, telling us your favourite Our Canadian Girl story, which parts you liked the most. Best of all, you told us which stories you would like to read, and we were amazed! There are so many remarkable stories in Canadian history. It seems that wherever we live, great stories live too, in our towns and cities, on our rivers and mountains. Thank you so much for sharing them.

So please, stay in touch. Write letters, log on to our website, let us know what you think of Our Canadian Girl. We're listening.

Sincerely,
Barbara Berson

Canada's

1608
Samuel de Champlain establishes the first fortified trading post at Quebec.

1759
The British defeat the French in the Battle of the Plains of Abraham.

1812
The United States declares war against Canada.

1845
The expedition of Sir John Franklin to the Arctic ends when the ship is frozen in the pack ice; the fate of its crew remains a mystery.

1869
Louis Riel leads his Métis followers in the Red River Rebellion.

1871
British Columbia joins Canada.

1755
The British expel the entire French population of Acadia (today's Maritime provinces), sending them into exile.

1776
The 13 Colonies revolt against Britain, and the Loyalists flee to Canada.

1837
Calling for responsible government, the Patriotes, following Louis-Joseph Papineau, rebel in Lower Canada; William Lyon Mackenzie leads the uprising in Upper Canada.

1867
New Brunswick, Nova Scotia and the United Province of Canada come together in Confederation to form the Dominion of Canada.

1870
Manitoba joins Canada. The Northwest Territories become an official territory of Canada.

1784
Rachel

Timeline

1885
At Craigellachie, British Columbia, the last spike is driven to complete the building of the Canadian Pacific Railway.

1898
The Yukon Territory becomes an official territory of Canada.

1914
Britain declares war on Germany, and Canada, because of its ties to Britain, is at war too.

1918
As a result of the Wartime Elections Act, the women of Canada are given the right to vote in federal elections.

1945
World War II ends conclusively with the dropping of atomic bombs on Hiroshima and Nagasaki.

1873
Prince Edward Island joins Canada.

1896
Gold is discovered on Bonanza Creek, a tributary of the Klondike River.

1905
Alberta and Saskatchewan join Canada.

1917
In the Halifax harbour, two ships collide, causing an explosion that leaves more than 1,600 dead and 9,000 injured.

1939
Canada declares war on Germany seven days after war is declared by Britain and France.

1949
Newfoundland, under the leadership of Joey Smallwood, joins Canada.

1896
Emily

1918
Penelope

1885
Marie-Claire

Check out the
Our Canadian Girl website

Fun Stuff

- E-cards
- Prizes
- Activities
- Poll

Fan Area

- Guest Book
- Photo Gallery
- Downloadable *Our Canadian Girl* Tea Party Kit

Features on the girls and more!

www.ourcanadiangirl.ca